I'll Be There

For my mum
A. S.

For Rebecca and Nora
M. P.

First published 2011 by Walker Books Ltd, 87 Vauxhall Walk, London SE11 5HJ ∘ 10 9 8 7 6 5 4 3 2 1 ∘ Text © 2011 Ann Stott ∘
Illustrations © 2011 Matt Phelan ∘ The right of Ann Stott and Matt Phelan to be identified as author and illustrator respectively of
this work has been asserted by them in accordance with the Copyright, Designs and Patents Act 1988 ∘ This book has been typeset
in Tempus Sans ITC ∘ Printed in China ∘ All rights reserved ∘ No part of this book may be reproduced, transmitted or stored in an
information retrieval system in any form or by any means, graphic, electronic or mechanical, including photocopying, taping and
recording, without prior written permission from the publisher ∘ British Library Cataloguing in Publication Data: a catalogue record for
this book is available from the British Library ∘ ISBN 978-1-4063-3177-6 ∘ www.walker.co.uk

I'll Be There

Ann Stott

illustrated by Matt Phelan

WALKER BOOKS
AND SUBSIDIARIES
LONDON · BOSTON · SYDNEY · AUCKLAND

Did you push me in a pram
when I was a baby?

Yes, I took you to the playground ...

and pushed you high on the swing.

I dressed you in stripes

and fed you mashed peas.

I gave you baths in the
kitchen sink

and wrapped you in your favourite
blanket to keep you warm.

When you were tired, I carried you up to bed

and read you your favourite bedtime story.

When you were a baby, I did lots
of things for you.

Now you can do them on your own.

I know. I can tie my own laces

and pick my own clothes.

I have showers now

and sometimes go to sleep after you!

I can read my own bedtime story

and even make breakfast for you!

Yes, you are growing up.

Will you still take care of me
when I'm big?

Well, you can tie your own laces and read your own bedtime story.

But I am your mum, and that will never change.

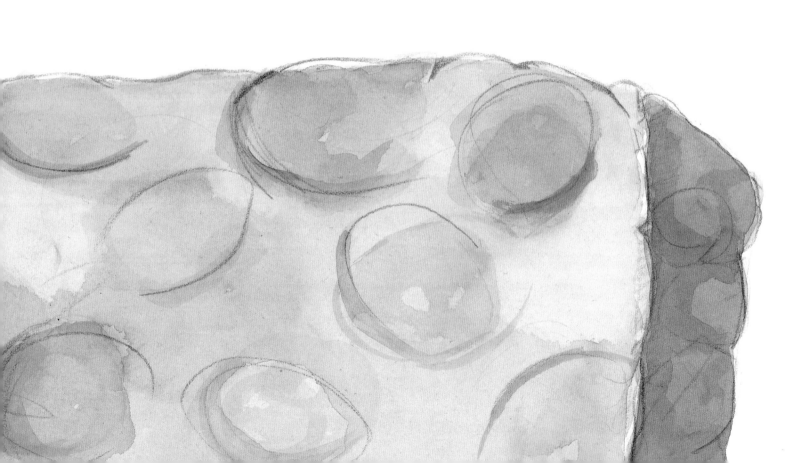

Even when you're big, I'll be there.